Spencer Hill Press

First Edition: May 2011.
Second Edition: June 2012.

Armentrout, Jennifer L. 1980
Daimon: The Prequel to Half-Blood : a novella/ by Jennifer L. Armentrout – 2nd ed.
p. cm.

Summary:
Seventeen-year-old Alexandria isn't a normal girl. She and her mother have been on the run for years – and what's looking for them isn't exactly human.

Cover design by K. Kaynak

ISBN 978-0-9831572-5-0 (paperback)
ISBN 978-0-9831572-6-7 (e-book)

Printed in the United States of America

Daimon

The Prequel to Half-Blood by

Jennifer L. Armentrout

SPENCER HILL PRESS

The *Covenant* Series

Pronunciation Guide for *Daimon*

Daimon: DEE-mun
Aether: EE-ther
Hematoi: HEM-a-toy

Before

CHAPTER 1

SHE SMELLED LIKE MOTHBALLS AND DEATH.

The elderly Hematoi Minister facing me looked like she had just crawled out of the tomb she'd been stored in for a couple hundred years. Her skin was wrinkled and thin, like old parchment, and each breath she took I swore would be her last. I hadn't ever seen anyone that old, but of course I'd only been seven and even the pizza guy had seemed ancient to me.

The crowd murmured its disapproval behind me; I'd forgotten that simple half-bloods like me weren't supposed to look a Minister in the eye. Being the pure-blood spawn of demigods, the Hematoi had huge egos.

I looked at my mother, who stood beside me on the raised dais. She was one of the Hematoi, but she wasn't anything like them. Her green eyes flashed a pleading look to cooperate, to not be the incorrigible and disobedient little girl she knew I could be.

I didn't know why she was so frightened; I was the one facing the crypt keeper. And if I survived this poor excuse for tradition without ending up carrying this hag's bedpan for the rest of my life, it would be a miracle worthy of the gods that supposedly were watching over all of us.

"Alexandria Andros?" The Minister's voice sounded like sandpaper over rough wood. She clucked her tongue. "She is far too small. Her arms are as thin as the shoots of new olive branches." She bent over to study me more closely, and I half expected her to fall in my face. "And her eyes, they are the color of dirt, hardly remarkable. She barely has any blood of the Hematoi in her. She is more mortal than any we have seen this day."

The Minister's eyes were the color of the sky before a violent storm. They were a mixture of purple and blue, a sign of her heritage. All the Hematoi had startling eye colors. Most of the half-bloods did too, but for some reason I'd missed the whole cool eye color boat when I'd been born.

The statements had continued on for what seemed like forever to me and all I could think about was ice cream and maybe taking a nap. Other Ministers had come down to check me over, whispering to each other as they circled me. I kept glancing at my mother and she'd smile reassuringly, letting me know that all of this was normal and that I was doing okay—great, even.

That was, until the old lady started pinching every piece of my exposed skin and then some. I'd always had this thing about being touched. If I didn't touch someone then I believed they shouldn't touch me. Grandma had apparently missed that memo.

She'd reached out and pinched my belly through my dress with her bony fingers. "She has no meat on her. How can we expect her to fight and defend us? She is not worthy to train at the Covenant and serve beside the children of the gods."

I'd never seen a god, but my mom told me there were always among us, always watching. I'd also never seen a pegasus or a chimera, but she'd sworn they also existed. Even at seven I'd had a hard time believing the stories; it had strained my fledgling faith to accept that the gods still cared about the world they had so diligently populated with their children in a way only the gods could.

"She's nothing more than a pathetic, little half-blood," the ancient woman had continued. "I say send her to the Masters. I'm in need of a little girl to clean my toilets."

Then she had twisted her fingers cruelly.

And I had kicked her shin.

I'd never forget the look on my mother's face, like she'd been caught between terror and full-blown panic, ready to run between them and snatch me away. There were a few gasps of outrage, but there were also a few deep chuckles.

"She has fire," one of the male Ministers had said. Another stepped forward, "She will do fine as a Guard, maybe even a Sentinel."

To this day I had no idea how I'd proved my worthiness after kicking the Minister in the leg. But I had. Not that it meant a damn thing now that I was seventeen and had been nowhere near the Hematoi world for the last three years. Even in the normal world I hadn't stopped doing stupid things.

Actually, I was prone to random acts of stupidity. I considered it to be one of my talents.

"You're doing it again, Alex." Matt's hand tightened around mine.

I blinked slowly, bringing his face into focus. "Doing what?"

"You got this look on your face." He tugged me against his chest, snaking an arm around my waist. "It's like you're thinking about something universally deep. Like your head is a thousand miles away, somewhere up in the clouds, on a different planet or something."

Matt Richardson wanted to join Greenpeace and save some whales. He was the pretty boy next door who'd sworn off eating red meat. Whatever. He was my current attempt to blend with the mortals, and he'd convinced me to sneak out and go to a bonfire on the beach with a bunch of people I barely knew.

I had bad taste in boys.

Previously, I'd crushed on a brooding academic who'd written poems on the back of his school books and styled his dyed, jet black hair so it'd covered his hazel eyes. He'd written a song about me. I'd laughed, and that relationship had been over before it got started. The year before that was probably my most embarrassing—the bleached blond, JV football captain with sky blue eyes. Months had gone by with us barely exchanging a "hey" and "do you have a pencil?" before we'd finally met up at a party. We'd talked. He'd kissed me and mauled my boobs, all the while smelling like cheap beer. I'd punched him and broken his jaw. Mom had moved me to a different town after that and lectured me about not hitting as hard as I could, reminding me that a normal girl couldn't throw punches like that.

Normal girls didn't want their boobs mauled either, and I wholly believed if they could've landed a fist like I could, they would have.

I smiled up at Matt. "I'm not thinking about anything."

"You're not thinking at all?" Matt lowered his head. The edges of his blond hair tickled my cheeks. Thank the gods he'd gotten over the "trying to grow dreads" stage in his life. "Nothing going on in that pretty head of yours?"

Something was going on in my head, but it wasn't what Matt hoped for. As I stared into his green eyes, I thought about my very first crush—the forbidden, older guy with thundercloud eyes—the one so far out of my league he might as well have been a different species.

Technically, I guess he was.

Even now, I wanted to spin-kick myself in my face for that one. I was like a walking romance novel character, thinking love conquers everything and all that crap. Sure. Love in my world usually ended up with someone hearing "I smite thee!" as she was cursed to be some lame flower for the rest of her life.

The gods and their children could be petty like that.

I sometimes wondered if my mom had sensed my budding obsession with the pure-blood guy and that was why she'd yanked my happy butt out of the only world I'd known—the only world I really belonged to. Pures were so off limits to halfs like me.

"Alex?" Matt brushed his lips over my cheek, moving ever so slowly toward my lips.

"Well, maybe something." I lifted up onto the tips of my toes and circled my arms around his neck. "Can you guess what I'm thinking about right now?"

"That you wish you hadn't left your shoes back at the fire, because I do. The sand is really cold. Global warming is a bitch."

"Not what I had in mind."

He frowned. "You're not thinking about history class, are you? That would be kind of lame, Alex."

I wiggled out of his grasp, sighing. "Never mind, Matt."

Chuckling, he reached out and wrapped his arms back around me. "I'm just kidding."

Doubtful, but I let him lower his lips to mine. His mouth was warm and dry, the most a girl could ask from a seventeen-year-old boy. But to be fair, Matt was a pretty damn good kisser. His lips moved against mine slowly and when he parted them, I didn't sock him in the stomach or anything like that. I returned the kiss.

Matt's hands dropped to my hips and he eased me down in the sand, supporting himself with one arm as he hovered over me and trailed kisses over my chin, down my throat. I stared up at the dark sky riddled with bright stars and very few clouds. A beautiful night—a normal night, I realized. There was something romantic about all of it, in the way he cradled my cheek when his mouth returned to mine and whispered my name like I was some kind of mystery he'd never be able to figure out. I felt warm and pleasant, not rip-my-clothes-off-and-do-me excited, but this wasn't bad. I could get used to this. Especially when I closed my eyes and pictured Matt's eyes turning gray and his hair much, much darker.

Then he slipped his hand under the hem of my sundress.

My eyes snapped open and I quickly reached down, pulling his hand out from between my legs. "Matt!"

"What?" He lifted his head, his eyes a murky green. "Why'd you stop me?"

Why had I stopped him? I suddenly felt like Miss Purity Princess guarding her virginity from wayward boys. Why? The answer actually came to me pretty quickly. I didn't want to give up my V-card on a beach with sand finding its way into unseemly places. My legs already felt like they'd been well exfoliated.

But it was more than that. I really wasn't in the here and now with Matt, not when I was picturing him with gray eyes and dark hair, wanting him to be someone else.

Someone I would never see again… and could never have.

CHAPTER 2

"ALEX?" MATT NUZZLED A SPOT ON MY NECK. "WHAT'S wrong?"

Using a bit of my natural strength, I rolled him off me and sat up. I readjusted the top of my dress, thankful for the darkness. "Sorry. I'm just not into it right now."

Matt remained sprawled beside me, staring up at the sky like I had moments before. "Did… did I do something wrong?"

My stomach twisted and felt funny. Matt was such a nice guy. I turned to him, grabbing his hand. I threaded my fingers through his, the way he liked it. "No. Not at all."

He pulled his hand free and rubbed it across his brow. "You always do this."

I frowned. Did I?

"It's not just that." Matt sat up, dropping his long arms over his bent knees. "I don't feel like I know you, Alex. You know, like really know who you are. And we've been dating how long?"

"A couple of months." I hoped that was correct. Then I felt like a douche for taking a guess. Gods, I was turning into a terrible person.

A small smile pulled at his lips. "You know everything about me. How old I was when I got into a club for the first time. What college I want to go to. The foods I hate and how I can't stand carbonated drinks. The first time I broke a bone—"

"Falling off your skateboard." I felt good about remembering that.

Matt laughed softly. "Yeah, you're right. But I don't know anything about you."

I nudged him with my shoulder. "That's not true."

"It is." He glanced at me, the smile on his face fading. "You don't ever talk about yourself."

Okay. He had a point, but it wasn't like I could tell him anything. I could see me now. Guess what? You ever watch Clash of the Titans or read any Greek fables? Well, those gods are real and yeah, I'm sort of a descendant of them. Kind of like the stepchild no one wants to claim. Oh, and I hadn't even been around mortals until three years ago. Can we still be friends?

Not going to happen.

So I shrugged and said, "There's really isn't anything to tell. I'm pretty boring."

Matt sighed. "I don't even know where you're from."

"I moved here from Texas. I've told you that." Strands of hair kept escaping my hand, blowing across my face and over his shoulder. I needed a haircut. "It's not a big secret."

"But were you born there?"

I looked away, watching the ocean. The sea was so dark it looked purple and unfriendly. I pulled my gaze away and stared down the shore. Two figures walked along, clearly male. "No," I said finally.

"Then where were you born?"

I fought the soft touch of annoyance as I focused on the guys near the shore, hunkered down as the wind picked up, pelting them with a fine sheen of cold water. A storm was coming.

"Alex?" Matt climbed to his feet, shaking his head. "See? You can't even tell me where you were born. What's up with that?"

My mom thought that the less people knew about us the better. She was incredibly paranoid, believing if anybody knew too much then the Covenant would find us. Was that such a bad thing? I kind of wanted them to find us, to put an end to this craziness.

Growing frustrated, Matt dragged his fingers through his hair. "I think I'm just going to head back to the group."

I watched him turn around before I scrambled to my feet. "Wait."

He turned around, brows raised.

I took a shallow breath, then another. "I was born on this stupid island no one has ever heard of. It's off the coast of North Carolina."

Surprise flickered across his features and he took a step toward me. "What island?"

"Seriously, you wouldn't have heard of it." I folded my arms over my chest as goosebumps crawled over my skin. "It's near Bald Head Island."

A wide smile spread across his face, and I knew the skin around his eyes was crinkling like it did whenever he was exceptionally happy about something. "Was that so hard?"

"Yes." I pouted and then smiled, because Matt had the kind of smile that was infectious, a smile that reminded me of the best friend I hadn't seen in years. Maybe that's why I was drawn to Matt. My own grin started to fade as I wondered what my former partner in mayhem was doing right now.

Matt dropped his hands on my arms, slowly uncrossing them. "Wanna head back?" He nodded down the beach, at the group of kids clustered around the bonfire. "Or stay here...?"

He'd left the offer open, but I knew what he meant. Stay here and kiss some more, forget some more. It didn't sound like a bad idea. I swayed toward him. Over his shoulder, I spotted the two guys again. They were almost on us and I sighed, now recognizing them.

"We have company." I stepped back.

Matt glanced over his shoulder at the two guys. "Great. It's Ren and Stimpy."

I giggled at the accurate description. During the few times I'd actually met the gruesome twosome, I refused to learn their real names. Ren was tall and lanky, his dark brown hair so full of hair gel it could be labeled a dangerous weapon in most states. Stimpy was the shorter and wider of the two, shaved bald and built like a locomotive. The two were known for causing trouble wherever they went, especially Stimpy and his questionable weightlifting program. They were two years older than us, having graduated from Matt's high school before I even stepped foot in Florida. But they still hung out with the younger crowd, no doubt scoping out impressionable girls. There'd been some bad rumors about those two.

Even in the pale moonlight I could tell their skin was a healthy shade of orange. Their overly broad smiles were obscenely white. The shorter one whispered something and they fist bumped each other.

Not unexpectedly, I didn't like them.

"Hey!" Ren called out as the pair's swagger slowed down. "What's up, Matt, my man?"

Matt shoved his hands in the pockets of his cargo shorts. "Nothing much—you?"

Ren glanced at Stimpy, then back to Matt. Ren's neon pink polo shirt looked painted on his scrawny frame, at least three sizes too small. "We're just chillin'. Gonna head out to the clubs later." Ren looked at me for the first time, his eyes drifting over my dress and down my legs.

I puked a little in my mouth.

"I've seen you around a few times," Ren said, bobbing his head to and fro. I wondered if it was some kind of weird mating dance. "What's your name, sweetness?"

"Her name's Alex," answered Stimpy in all his shifty eyed glory. "It's a guy's name."

I stifled my groan. "My mom wanted a boy."

Ren looked confused.

"Actually it's short for Alexandria," Matt explained. "She just likes to be called Alex."

I grinned at Matt, but he was watching the two guys closely. A muscle feathered along his jaw.

"Thanks for the clarification, bud." Stimpy crossed his massive arms, eyeballing Matt.

Catching Stimpy's look, I shifted closer to Matt.

Ren, still staring at my legs, made a sound that was a cross between a grunt and a moan. "Damn girl. Is your daddy a thief?"

"What?" I'd never actually met my dad. Maybe he was. All I knew was that he'd been mortal. Hopefully, he'd been nothing like these two ass-hats.

Ren flexed his nonexistent muscles, smiling. "Well, then who stole those diamonds and put them in your eyes?"

"Wow." I blinked and turned to Matt. "Why don't you ever say such romantic stuff like that to me, Matt? I'm hurt."

Matt didn't grin like I expected. His gaze kept bouncing between the two, and I could see his hands balling into fists inside his pockets. There was a certain edge to his eyes, to the way his lips were drawn into a tight line. My amusement vanished in an instant. He was… scared?

I reached for Matt's arm. "Come on, let's head back."

"Wait." Stimpy clapped Matt on the shoulder with enough force to cause Matt to stumble backward a few inches. "Kind of rude of you guys to just run off."

A rush of warm air crawled up my spine and spread over my skin. My muscles tensed with anticipation. "Don't touch him," I warned softly.

Out of surprise, Stimpy dropped his hand and stared at me. Then he smiled. "She's a bossy one."

"Alex," Matt hissed, staring at me with wide eyes. "It's okay. Don't make a big deal out of it."

He hadn't seen me make a big deal yet.

"The 'tude must come with the name." Ren laughed. "Why don't we go party? I know a bouncer down at Zero who can get us in. We all can have a good time." Then he grabbed for me.

Ren may have meant to do it playfully, but it was seriously the wrong move. I still had a serious issue with being touched when I didn't want to be. I caught his arm. "Was your mom a gardener?" I asked innocently.

"What?" Ren's mouth hung open slightly.

"Because a face like yours belongs planted on the ground." I twisted his arm back. Shock flickered over his features. There was a second when our gazes locked, and I could tell he wasn't sure how I'd gained the upper hand so quickly.

It had been three years since I'd seriously fought anyone, but unused muscles woke up and my brain sort of clicked off. I dipped under the arm I held, bringing it along with me as I clipped his knee with my foot.

The next second Ren ate sand.

CHAPTER 3

STARING DOWN AT THE GUY SPRAWLED SPREAD-EAGLE in the sand, I realized I kind of missed fighting, especially the rush of adrenaline and the "Damn, I rock" feeling that came along with taking someone down. But then again, fighting mortals was nothing like fighting my own kind or the things I'd once trained to kill. This had been effortless. If he'd been another half-blood, I might've been the one with a mouthful of sand looking pretty damn lame.

"Jesus," Matt whispered, jumping back.

I looked up, expecting to see a shock and awe kind of look from him. Maybe even a thumbs up. Nothing, I got nothing from him. At the Covenant, I would've been applauded. But I kept forgetting I wasn't at the Covenant anymore.

Stimpy's dumbstruck gaze swung from his pal to me and quickly turned to fury. "You act like a man? You better be able to take it like a man, you bitch."

"Oh." I smiled as I faced him fully. "It's on like Donkey Kong."

Having the obvious body mass thing going for him, Stimpy rushed me. But he hadn't been trained to fight from the age of seven and he didn't have my literally god-given strength and speed. He swung a meaty fist toward my face and I spun around, kicking out and planting my bare foot in his stomach. Stimpy doubled over, throwing out his hands as he tried to capture my arms. I stepped into him, grabbing his upper arms and yanking him down as I brought my leg up. His jaw bounced off my knee and I let go, watching him fall into the sand with a grunt.

Ren stumbled to his feet, spitting out sand. He swayed and then took a swing at me. It was way off, and I could have easily dodged it. Hell, I could've stood still and he wouldn't have made contact, but I was on a roll now.

I caught his fist, sliding my hand down his arm. "Hitting girls isn't nice." I turned around, using his body weight to knock him off balance. He went over my shoulder, face first into the sand once more.

Stimpy climbed to his feet and staggered to his fallen friend. "Come on, man. Get up."

"Need help?" I offered with a sweet smile.

Both guys scrambled down the beach, looking over their shoulders like they expected me to jump on their backs. I watched them until they disappeared around the cove, smiling to myself.

I turned back to Matt, the wind blowing my hair around me. I felt alive for the first time in... well, years. I can still kick ass. After all this time, I can still do it. My excitement and confidence dried up and shriveled away the moment I got a good look at Matt's face.

He looked horrified. "How...?" He cleared his throat. "Why did you do that?"

"Why?" I repeated, confused. "It seems pretty clear to me. Those guys are dicks."

"Yes, they're dicks. Everyone knows that, but you didn't have to lay the smackdown on them." Matt stared at me, eyes wide. "I just... I just can't believe you did that."

"They were bothering you!" I planted my hands on my hips, past caring about the wind smacking my hair in my face. "Why are you acting like I'm some kind of freak?"

"All they did is touch me, Alex."

That was enough reason for me, but apparently, not enough for Matt. "Ren grabbed at me. I'm sorry. I'm not down with that."

Matt just stared at me.

I bit back the string of curse words that were forming in my mind. "Okay. Maybe I shouldn't have done all that. Can we just forget about it?"

"No." He rubbed the back of his neck. "That was too weird for me. Sorry Alex, but that was just... freaky."

My ever tenuous hold on my anger started to thin. "Oh, so next time you want me to stand here and let them kick your ass and molest me?"

"You overreacted! They weren't going to kick my ass or molest you! And there won't be a next time. I'm not down with violence." Matt shook his head and turned away from me, plowing his feet through the mounds of sand, leaving me standing all alone.

"What the hell?" I muttered and then louder, "Whatever! Go save a dolphin or something!"

He whirled around. "It's a whale, Alex, a whale! That's what I'm interested in saving."

I threw up my arms. "What's wrong with saving dolphins?"

Matt ignored me at that point, and about two minutes later, I truly regretted yelling that. I stormed past him to retrieve my sandals and bag, but I did so with grace and dignity. Not one single disparaging remark or cuss word escaped my tightly sealed lips.

A couple of kids glanced up, but none of them said anything. The few friends I had at school had been Matt's friends, and they liked saving whales too. Not that anything was wrong with saving whales, but some of them threw their beer bottles and plastic wrappers in the ocean. Hypocritical much?

Matt just didn't understand. Violence was a part of who I was as a half-blood, ingrained in my blood since birth and trained into every muscle in my body. It didn't mean I was going to snap and body slam someone for no good reason, but I would fight back. Always.

The walk home sucked butt.

I had sand between my toes, in my hair and up my dress. My skin chafed in all the wrong places and everything freaking sucked. Looking back, I could admit that I might've overreacted a tad. Ren and Stimpy hadn't been particularly threatening. I could've just let it slide. Or acted like a normal girl in the situation and let Matt handle it.

But I hadn't.

I never did. Now everything was going to be screwed up. Matt would go to school on Monday and tell everyone how I'd gone Xena Warrior Princess on the douchebags. I'd have to tell my mom, and she would freak. Maybe she'd insist we move again. I'd actually be happy about that; there was no way I could go back to school and face those kids after Matt told them what'd happened. I didn't care that school would be ending in a few weeks, anyway. I also wasn't looking forward to the major bitch-fest coming my way.

One I knew I deserved.

Clenching the little purse in my fist, I picked up my pace. Normally the neon lights from the clubs and the sounds of the nearby carnival put me in a happy mood, but not tonight. I wanted to punch myself in the face.

We lived three blocks off the beach, in a two story bungalow Mom rented from some ancient guy who smelled like sardines. It was kind of old, but it had two tiny bathrooms. Bonus points there—we didn't have to share. It wasn't exactly in the safest neighborhood known to man, but an iffy side of town wasn't anything that would scare my mom or me.

Bad mortals we could handle.

I sighed as I navigated the still crowded boardwalk. The nightlife was a big thing here. So were fake ID's and super-tan, super-skinny bodies. Everyone looked alike to me in Miami, which wasn't very different from my home—my real home—where I'd once had a purpose in life, a duty I'd be obligated to fulfill.

And now I was pretty much a loser.

I'd lived in four different cities and attended four high schools in three years. We always picked large cities to disappear in and always lived near water. So far we'd only attracted a little attention, and when we had, we'd run. Never once did my mom tell me why, not even a single explanation. After the first year, I'd stopped getting mad when she wouldn't tell me why she'd come to my dorm room that night and told me we had to leave. I'd honestly given up asking and trying to figure it out. Sometimes I hated her for all of this, but she was my mom and where she went, I went.

Dampness settled in the air, the sky overhead quickly darkening until no stars shone down. I crossed the narrow street and kicked open the gate of the waist-high, wrought iron fence surrounding our little patch of grass. I winced at the screech as it swung open, scraping along the sandstone pavers.

I stopped in front of the door, looking up as I searched my purse for the key. "Crap," I muttered as my eyes roamed over the little garden balcony. Flowers and herbs grew like crazy, overflowing their ceramic pots and climbing the rusty railings. Empty urns I'd stacked in a pile weeks ago had toppled over. I was supposed to have cleaned up the balcony this afternoon.

Mom was going to be pissed for a lot of reasons in the morning.

Sighing, I pulled out the key and shoved it in the lock. I had the door halfway open, thankful it hadn't creaked and groaned like everything else in the house did, when I felt the most unfamiliar sensation.

Icy fingers ran up my spine, and then down. All the tiny hairs on my body stood up as the unerring sense of being watched came over me.

CHAPTER 4

I QUICKLY TURNED, MY GAZE DARTING OVER THE little yard and beyond. The streets were empty, but the feeling only increased. Unease gnawed at my stomach as I stepped back and reached behind me, wrapping my fingers around the edge of the door. Nobody was there, but…

"I'm losing my mind," I muttered. "I'm getting as paranoid as Mom. Nice."

I went inside, locking the door behind me. The uncanny feeling slowly eased off as I tiptoed through the silent house. I inhaled and nearly gagged on the spicy aroma filling the living room.

Groaning, I turned on the lamp beside the secondhand, shabby couch and squinted into the corner of the room. Sitting beside our TV and the magazine rack full of US Weekly was Apollo. A fresh wreath of bay laurel wrapped around the marble cast of his head. Of all the things my mom had forgotten to pack the many times we moved, she'd never forgotten him.

I loathed the statue of Apollo and his stinky bay laurel wreath my mom replaced every godsforsaken day of my life. Not because I had anything against Apollo. I guessed he was a pretty cool god since he was all about harmony, order and reason. It was just the gaudiest damn thing I'd ever seen in my life.

It was only the bust of his chest and head, but engraved across his chest were a lyre, a dolphin, and—if that wasn't enough symbolic overload for the masses—there were a dozen tiny cicadas perched on his shoulder. What the hell did the annoying, buzzing insects that got stuck in people's hair even stand for? Symbolizing music and song my rosy left butt cheek.

I'd never understood my mom's fascination with Apollo or with any of the gods for that matter. They'd been on the absentee list since mortals had decided sacrificing their virgin daughters was a totally uncool practice. I didn't know a soul who'd ever seen a god. They'd run around and bred a hundred or so demigods and then let them have babies—the pure-bloods—but they never showed up on anyone's birthday bearing gifts.

Holding my hand over my nose, I walked over to the candle surrounded by more laurel and blew it out. Being a god of prophecy, I wondered if Apollo had foreseen that. Gaudiness aside, what was shown of his marble chest was pretty nice.

Nicer than Matt's chest.

Which was something I'd never be seeing or touching again. With that in mind, I grabbed the carton of double chocolate fudge ice cream out of the freezer and a large spoon. Not even bothering with a bowl, I climbed the uneven steps.

Soft light spilled out from the gap between my mom's bedroom door and the floor. Stopping in front of her door, I glanced at my room and then down at the ice cream. I bit my lower lip and debated bursting into her room. She probably already knew I'd snuck out earlier and if she didn't, the sand covering half my body would give it away. But I hated the fact that my mom was home alone on a Friday night. Again.

"Lexie?" The soft and sweet voice called from behind the door. "What are you doing?"

I nudged open the door and peeked inside. She sat at the head of the bed, reading one of those smutty romance novels with half-naked guys on the cover. I totally stole them when she wasn't looking. Beside her on the small bedside table was a pot of hibiscus flowers. They were her favorite. The purple petals were beautiful, but the only scent came from the vanilla oil she loved to sprinkle over the petals.

She looked up, a slight smile on her face. "Hi, honey. Welcome home."

I held up my carton of ice cream, cringing. "At least I'm home before midnight."

"Is that supposed to make it okay?" She pinned me with a look, her emerald eyes glittering in the dim light.

"No?"

My mom sighed, setting her novel down. "I know you want to go out and be with your friends, especially since you started seeing that boy. What's his name? Mike?"

"Matt." My shoulders slumped and I eyed the ice cream eagerly. "His name is Matt."

"Matt. That's right." She gave me a brief smile. "He's a really nice boy, and I understand you want to be with him, but I don't want you running around Miami at night, Lexie. It's not safe."

"I know."

"I've never had to… what do they call it? When privileges are suspended?"

"Grounding." I tried not to smile. "They call it grounding."

"Ah, yes. I've never had to 'ground' you, Lexie. I really don't want to start now." She brushed back the thick, wavy brown hair from her face as her gaze drifted over me. "Why in the name of the gods are you covered in sand?"

I inched inside her room. "It's a long story."

If she suspected I'd rolled around in the sand with the boy whose name she kept forgetting and then kung foo'd my way through two other guys, she didn't let on. "Want to talk about it?"

I shrugged.

She patted the bed. "Come on, baby."

Feeling a bit dejected, I sat and tucked my legs under me. "I'm sorry about sneaking out."

Her bright gaze dropped to the ice cream. "I believe you may be wishing you'd stayed home?"

"Yeah." I sighed, cracking open the lid and digging in. Around a mouthful of ice cream, I said, "Matt and I are no more."

"I thought his name was Mitch?"

I rolled my eyes. "No, Mom, his name is Matt."

"What happened?"

Looking at her was like staring in the mirror, except I was more like a mundane version of her. Her cheekbones were sharper, her nose a little smaller, and her lips more lush than mine. And she had those amazing green eyes. It was the mortal blood in me that watered down my appearance. I'm sure my dad must've been hotness to have caught my mom's married eye, but he had been very human. Hooking up with humans wasn't prohibited by any means, mainly because the children—half-bloods like me—were extremely valuable assets to the pures. Well, I couldn't be included as an asset any longer.

Now I was just… I didn't know what I was anymore.

"Lexie?" She leaned forward, snatching the spoon and carton from my hands. "I'll eat and you tell me what the idiot boy did."

I smiled. "It's all my fault."

She swallowed a mammoth chunk of ice cream. "As your mother I am obligated to disagree."

"Oh, no." I flopped on my back and stared up at the ceiling fan. "You're going to change your mind on that one."

"Let me be the judge of that."

I scrubbed my hands over my face. "Well, I kind of… got into a fight with two guys on the beach."

"What?" I felt the bed shift as she straightened. "What did they do? Did they try to hurt you? Did they… touch you inappropriately?"

"Oh! Gods no, Mom, come on." I dropped my hands, frowning at her. "It wasn't like that. Not really."

Thick strands of hair blew back from her face. Simultaneously all the curtains in the room lifted, reaching toward the bed. The book beside her flew off the bed and landed somewhere on the floor. "What happened, Alexandria?"

I sighed. "Nothing like that, Mom. Okay? Calm down before you blow us out of our own home."

She stared at me a few moments, and then the winds died down.

"Show-off," I muttered. Pure-bloods like my mom could command one of the elements, a gift the gods had bestowed upon the Hematoi. Mom had a thing for the element of air, but she wasn't very good at controlling it. Once she blew over a neighbor's car—try explaining that to the insurance company. "These guys started messing with Matt and one of them grabbed at me."

"Then what happened?" Her voice sounded calm.

I prepared myself. "Well, they kind of needed to help each other off the ground."

My mom didn't immediately respond to that. I dared a quick look at her and found her expression relatively blank. "How bad?"

"They're fine." I smoothed my hands down the front of my dress. "I didn't even hit them. Well, I kicked one of them. But he called me a bitch, so I think he deserved it. Anyway, Matt said I overreacted and he wasn't into violence. He looked at me like I was a freak."

"Lexie…"

"I know." I sat up and rubbed the back of my neck. "I did overreact. I could've just walked away or whatever. Now Matt doesn't want to see me anymore and all the kids are going to think I'm some kind of… I don't know, weirdo."

"You're not a weirdo, baby."

I gave her a droll look. "There's a statue of Apollo in our living room. And come on, I'm not even the same species as them."

"You're not a different species." She dropped the spoon in the carton. "You're more like the mortals than you realize."

"I don't know about that." I crossed my arms, scowling. After a few seconds, I glanced at her. "Aren't you going to yell at me or something?"

She arched a brow and seemed to consider it. "I think you've learned that action is not always the best response, and the boy called you such an ugly name…"

A slow grin pulled at my lips. "They were total douchebags. I swear."

"Lexie!"

"What?" I giggled at her expression. "They are. And douchebag isn't a cuss word."

She shook her head. "I don't even want to know what it is, but it sounds revolting."

I giggled again, but sobered up when Matt's horrified face flashed before me. "You should have seen the way Matt looked at me afterward. It was like he was afraid of me. So stupid. You know? Kids like me would have applauded that, but no, Matt had to look at me like I was the antichrist on crack."

My mom's brows puckered. "I'm sure it wasn't that bad."

The painting of a goddess on her wall became a sole focus to me. Artemis crouched beside a doe, a quiver of silver arrows in one hand and a bow in the other. The eyes were unnerving, painted completely white—no irises or pupils. "No. It was. He thinks I'm a freak."

She scooted closer, placing a gentle hand on my knee. "I know it's hard for you to be away from… the Covenant, but you'll be okay. You'll see. You have your whole life ahead of you, full of choice and freedom."

Ignoring that comment and wherever it came from, I took back my ice cream and shook the empty carton. "Boo, Mom, you ate it all."

"Lexie." Cupping my cheek, she turned my head so I faced her. "I know it bothers you being away from there. I know you want to go back and I pray to the gods that you can find happiness in this new life. But we can never go back there. You know that, right?"

"I know," I whispered, even though I really didn't know why.

"Good." She pressed her lips to my cheek. "With or without a purpose, you're a very special girl. Don't ever forget that."

Something burned in the back of my throat. "You're like totally obligated to say that. You're my mom."

She laughed. "That is true."

"Mom!" I exclaimed. "Wow. Now I'm going to have self-esteem problems."

"That is one area you are not lacking in." She sent me a saucy grin as I smacked at her hand. "Now get off my bed and go to sleep. I expect you up bright and early. Your little butt better be out on that balcony, cleaning up that mess. I'm serious."

I hopped from the bed and shook my butt. "It's not that little."

Her eyes rolled. "Good night, Lexie."

I skipped to the door, glancing over my shoulder at her. She was patting the bed, frowning.

"Your windstorm knocked it on the floor." I went over and picked the book up, handing it to her. "G'night!"

"Lexie?"

"Yeah?" I turned back around.

My mom smiled and it was such a beautiful smile, warm and loving. It lit up her entire face, turning her eyes into jewels. "I love you."

I smiled. "Love you, too, Mom."

CHAPTER 5

AFTER DUMPING THE EMPTY CARTON AND WASHING off the spoon, I scrubbed my face and changed into a pair of old jammies. Restless, I tinkered around with the idea of cleaning my room, an impulse that lasted long enough for me to pick up a few socks.

I sat on the edge of the bed, staring at the shuttered balcony doors. The white paint was cracked, showing a deeper layer in a pale shade of gray—like a cross between blue and silver, an unusual shade that struck an old yearning inside me.

Really, after all this time, to still even think about a guy I'll never see again was freaking ridiculous. Worse yet, he hadn't even known I'd existed. Not because I'd been some kind of wallflower, wilting away in the shadows at the Covenant, but because he hadn't been allowed to notice me. Here I was, three years later, and chipping paint reminded me of his eyes.

That was so lame it was embarrassing.

Annoyed with my own thoughts, I pushed off the bed and went to the little desk in the corner of my room. Papers and notebooks I rarely used in class covered the top. If there was anything I loved about the mortal world, it was their school system. Classes out here were a piece of cake compared to what went on at the Covenant. Knocking the clutter to the side, I found my out of date MP3 player and earbuds.

Most people had cool music on their players: Indie bands or the current hits. I decided I must've been high on something—Apollo's bay laurel fumes?—when I'd downloaded these songs. I clicked through—that's how out of date this thing was—until I found Van Morrison's Brown Eyed Girl.

There was something about the song that turned me into a walking cheese ball from the very first guitar riff. Humming along, I danced around my room, picking up discarded clothing and stopping every few seconds to flail about. I threw the pile in the basket, bobbing my head like a deranged Muppet Baby.

Starting to feel a little better about things, I grinned as I shimmied around my bed, clutching a pile of socks to my chest. "Sha la la, la la, la la, la la, la-la tee da. La-la tee da!"

I winced at the sound of my own voice. Singing was not a personal strength, but that didn't stop me from mutilating every song on my MP3 player. By the time my room was fairly decent, it was past three in the morning. Exhausted but happy, I tugged out the earbuds and dropped them on the desk. Crawling into bed, I flipped off the lamp and dropped down. Usually it took me a while to drift off, but sleep came easily that night.

And because my brain liked to torture me even while I slept, I dreamt of Matt. But the dream-Matt had dark, wavy hair and eyes the color of storm clouds. And in the dream, when his hands roamed under my dress, I didn't stop him.

†

A strange, satisfied smile pulled at my lips when I awoke. I kicked back the covers, stretching lazily as my gaze fell on the balcony doors. Thin sheets of light broke through the creases under the shudders and slid over the old bamboo throw rug. Specks of dust floated and danced in the rays.

My smile froze when I spotted the clock. "Crap!"

Throwing the bedspread to the side, I swung my legs off the bed and stood. "Bright and early" did not translate to waking up at noon. My mom had gone easy on me last night, but I doubted she'd feel the same if I added not doing my chores for the second day in the row. A quick glimpse at my reflection in the tiny bathroom mirror while I stripped confirmed I looked like Chewbacca. I took a quick shower, but the hot water still went cold before I could finish.

Shivering from the wrath of the evil water heater, I changed into a pair of worn jeans and a loose shirt. Towel drying my hair, I started toward my door. I stopped, smothering a yawn. Mom was probably already outside in the tiny garden in the front. It was right below the balcony, facing the apartment buildings and row homes across the street. I tossed the towel on the bed and threw open the balcony doors like some kind of southern belle greeting the day, all ladylike and delicate.

Except it all went wrong.

Wincing from the glare of the bright Florida sun, I shielded my eyes and stepped forward. My foot snagged in an empty flowerpot. Trying to shake it off, I lost my balance and careened across the balcony, catching myself on the railing before I could topple over it headfirst.

Death by flowerpot would be a hell of a way to go.

Underneath my arms, the rickety-ass wooden plant stand swayed to the left and then the far, far right. Several pots of green and yellow tulips shifted all at once.

"Crap!" I hissed. Pushing off the railing and dropping to my knees, I hugged the plant stand to my chest. Kneeling there, for once I was grateful that none of my old friends had been around to see that.

Half-bloods were known for their agility and grace, not for tripping over things.

Once I got everything back to where it was supposed to be without killing myself in the process, I stood and leaned carefully over the railing. I scanned the flowerbeds, expecting to find Mom laughing her butt off, but the yard was empty. I even checked by the fence, where she had planted a row of flowers a few weekends ago. I started to turn back when I saw the gate was open, hanging to the side.

"Huh." I was almost positive I'd closed it last night. Maybe Mom had gone to the Krispy Kreme to get doughnuts? Mmm. My stomach grumbled. I grabbed the garden spade out of the mess of tools piled atop the small folding chair, bemoaning another morning eating shredded wheat if there weren't doughnuts. Who did I have to kill to get some Count Chocula up in this house?

I flipped the spade over in the air, catching it by the handle while I gazed past the yard. The row houses across the street all had bars on the windows and paint peeling off the sides. The old women who inhabited them didn't speak much English. Once I'd tried helping one of them pull her garbage bags out to the curb, but she'd yelled at me in another language and shooed me away like I'd been trying to steal it.

They were all out on their stoops right now, cutting coupons or doing whatever it was that old ladies did. Traffic packed the street. It was always like this on a Saturday afternoon, especially when it was turning out to be a nice day for a beach trip.

My gaze crawled over the townies and the tourists as I continued to toss the spade in the air. It was always easy to pick out the out-of-towners. They wore fanny packs or abnormally large sun hats and their skin was either fish pale or sunburned.

A strange shiver coursed over me, spreading tiny bumps over my flesh. I sucked in a sharp breath, my eyes scanning the passing crowds with a will of their own.

Then I saw it.

Everything stopped around me in an instant. The air went right out of my lungs.

No. No. No.

He stood at the mouth of the alley, directly across from the bungalow and right beside the front porch where the old ladies sat. They glanced over at him as he stepped out onto the sidewalk, but they dismissed the stranger and returned to their conversation.

They couldn't see what I saw.

No mortal could. Not even a pure-blood could. Only half-bloods could see through the elemental magic and witness the true horror—skin so pale and so thin that every vein popped through the flesh like a baby black snake. His eyes were dark, empty sockets and his mouth, his teeth…

This was one of the things I'd been trained to fight at the Covenant. This was a thing that thrived and fed on aether—the essence of the gods, the very life force running through us—a pure-blood who had turned his back on the gods. This was one of the things I was obligated to kill on sight.

A daimon—there was a daimon here.

CHAPTER 6

I WHEELED AWAY FROM THE RAILING. WHATEVER training I'd managed to retain vanished in an instant. Part of me had known—had always known—deep down that this day would come. We'd been outside the protection of the Covenant and their communities for far too long. The need for aether would eventually draw a daimon to our doorstep. Daimons couldn't resist the pure-blood mojo. I just hadn't wanted to give voice to the fear, to believe that it could happen on a day like this, when the sun was so bright and the sky such a beautiful azure blue.

Panic clawed at the inside of my throat, trapping my voice. I tried to yell, "Mom!" but it came out a hoarse whisper.

I rushed through the bedroom, terror seizing me as I pushed and then pulled open the door. A crash sounded from somewhere in the house. The space between my bedroom and my mom's seemed longer than I remembered and I was still trying to call out her name as I reached her room.

The door opened smoothly, but at the same time, everything slowed down.

Her name was still just a whimper on my lips. My gaze landed on her bed first, and then on a section of floor beside the bed. I blinked. The pot of hibiscus had toppled over and broken into large pieces. Purple petals and soil were strewn across the floor. Red—something red—mingled among the blossoms, turning them a deep violet. My gasp drew in a metallic smell that reminded me of the nose bleeds I used to get when a sparring partner would get in a lucky shot.

I shuddered.

Time stilled. A buzzing filled my ears until I couldn't hear anything else. I saw her hand first. Abnormally pale and open, her fingers clawed at the air, reaching for something. Her arm twisted at an awkward angle. My head shook back and forth; my brain refused to accept the images in front of my eyes, to name the dark stain spreading down her shirt.

No, no—absolutely no. This was wrong.

Something—someone—braced half her body up. A pale hand clenched her upper arm and her head lolled to the side. Her eyes were wide open, the green somewhat faded and unfocused.

Oh, gods… oh, gods.

Seconds, it had only been seconds since I'd opened the door, but it felt like forever.

A daimon was latched onto my mother, draining her to get at the aether in the blood. I must've made a sound, because the daimon's head lifted. Her neck—oh gods—her neck had been torn into. So much blood had been spilled.

My eyes met those of the daimon—or at least, they met the dark holes where its eyes should have been. His mouth snapped away from her neck, gaping open to reveal a row of razor-like teeth covered in blood. Then the elemental magic took over, piecing together the face he'd had as a pure, before he'd tasted that first drop of aether. With that glamour in place, he was beautiful by any standard—so much so that, for a moment, I thought I was seeing things. Nothing that angelic-looking could be responsible for the red stain on my mother's neck, her clothes…

His head tipped to the side as he sniffed the air. He let out a high-pitched keening sound. I stumbled backward. The sound—nothing real could sound like that.

He let go of my mom, letting her body slip to the floor. She fell in a messy heap and didn't move. I knew she had to be scared and hurt, because there couldn't be any other reason why she hadn't moved. Rising up, the daimon's bloody hands fell to his sides, fingers twisting inward.

His lips curved into a smile. "Half-blood," he whispered.

Then he jumped.

I didn't even realize I still held the garden spade. I raised my arm just as the daimon grabbed me. My scream came out as nothing more than a hoarse squeak as I fell back against the wall. The painting of Artemis crashed to the floor beside me.

The daimon's eyes widened with surprise. His irises were a vibrant, deep blue for a moment, and then, like a switch being thrown, the elemental magic that hid his true nature vanished. Black sockets replaced those eyes; veins popped through his whitish skin.

And then he exploded in a burst of shimmery blue powder.

I looked down dumbly at my trembling hand. The garden spade—I still held the freaking garden spade. Titanium-plated, I realized slowly. The spade had been coated in the metal deadly to those addicted to aether. Had my mom bought the ridiculously expensive garden tools because she loved to garden, or had there been an ulterior motive behind the purchase? It wasn't like we had any Covenant daggers or knives lying around.

Either way, the daimon had impaled itself on the spade. Stupid, evil, aether-sucking son of a bitch.

A laugh—short and rough—bubbled up my throat as a tremor ran through my body. There was nothing but silence and the world snapped back into place.

The spade slipped from my limp fingers, clattering on the floor. Another spasm sent me to my knees and I lowered my eyes to the unmoving form beside the bed.

"Mom...?" I winced at the sound of my voice and the shot of fear that went through me.

She didn't move.

I placed my hand on her shoulder and rolled her onto her back. Her head fell to the side, her eyes blank and unseeing. My gaze fell to her neck. Blood covered the front of her blue blouse and matted the strands of her dark hair. I couldn't tell how much damage had been done. I reached out again, but I couldn't bring myself to brush back the hair covering her neck. In her right hand, she'd clenched a crushed petal.

"Mom…?" I leaned over her, my heart stuttering and missing a beat. "Mom!"

She didn't even blink. During all of this, my brain was trying to tell me there was no life in those eyes, no spirit and no hope in her vacant stare. Tears ran down my face, but I couldn't recall when I'd started crying. My throat convulsed to the point I struggled to breathe.

I cried her name then, grabbing her arms and shaking her. "Wake up! You have to wake up! Please, Mom, please! Don't do this! Please!"

For a second I thought I saw her lips move. I bent down, placing my ear over her mouth, straining to hear one tiny breath, one word.

There was nothing.

Searching for some sign of life, I touched the undamaged side of her neck and then jerked back, falling on my butt. Her skin—her skin was so cold. I stared at my hands. They were covered with blood. Her skin was too cold. "No. No."

A door shut downstairs, and the sound broke through to me. I froze for a second, my heart racing so fast I was sure it would explode. A shudder passed through my frame as the image of the daimon outside flashed through my head. What color had his hair been? The one in here had been blond. What color?

"Hell." I scrambled to my feet and slammed the door shut. Fingers shaking, I turned the lock and whirled around.

There were two. There were two.

Heavy footsteps pounded on the stairs.

I rushed over to the dresser. Squeezing myself behind it, I shoved the heavy furniture with every ounce of strength I had in me. Books and papers toppled over as I blocked the door. Something slammed into the other side, shaking the dresser. Jumping back, I ran my hands over my head. A keening howl erupted from the other side of the door, and then it struck the door again… and again.

I whirled around, stomach twisting in painful knots. Plans—we had a stupid plan in place just in case a daimon found us. We modified it every time we moved to a different city, but each one boiled down to one thing: Get the money and run. I heard her voice as clear as if she had spoken it. Take the money and run. Don't look back. Just run.

The daimon hit the door again, splintering the wood. An arm snaked through, grasping at the air.

I went to the closet, pulling down boxes from the top shelf until a small wooden one fell to the floor. Grabbing it, I yanked it so fiercely that the lid ripped from the hinges. I threw another box at the door, hitting the daimon's arm. I think it laughed at me. I grabbed what my mom called the 'emergency fund' and what I referred to as the 'we are so screwed' fund and pocketed the wad of hundred dollar bills.

Every step back to where she had fallen ripped through me, taking a piece of my soul. I ignored the daimon as I dropped beside her and pressed my lips to her cool forehead. "I'm so sorry, Mom. I'm so sorry. I love you."

"I'm going to kill you," the daimon hissed.

Looking over my shoulder, I saw the daimon's head had made it through the door. He was reaching for the edge of the dresser. I picked up the garden spade, wiping the back of my arm over my face.

"I'm going to rip you apart. Do you hear me?" he continued, squeezing another arm through the hole he'd made. "Rip you open and drain you of whatever pathetic amount of aether you have, half-blood."

I glanced at the window and grabbed the lamp off the table. Tearing the shade off, I tossed it aside. I stopped in front of the dresser.

The daimon stilled as the glamour settled around him. He sniffed the air, eyes flaring wide. "You smell dif—"

Swinging with all my might, I slammed the bottom of the lamp into the daimon's head. The sickening thud it made pleased me in a way that would've concerned guidance counselors across the nation. It wouldn't kill him, but it sure as hell made me feel better.

I threw the busted lamp down and raced to the window. I pushed it open just as the daimon let out a string of creative cusses and threats. I wiggled into the window, perching there as I stared at the ground below, assessing my chances of landing on the awning over the small porch off the back of the house.

The part of me that had been in the mortal world too long balked at the idea of jumping from a second story window. The other part—the part that had the blood of the gods running through it—jumped.

The metal roof made a terrible sound when my feet slapped into it. I didn't think as I went to the edge and leapt once more. I hit the grass, falling to my knees. Pushing up, I ignored the stunned looks from the neighbors who must've come outside to see what was going on. I did the one thing I'd been trained never to do during my time at the Covenant, the thing I didn't want to do, but knew I had to.

I ran.

With my cheeks still damp with tears and my hands stained with my mother's blood, I ran.

After

CHAPTER 7

A DEEP NUMBNESS SETTLED OVER ME AS I STOOD IN A gas station bathroom. I turned my hands over and rubbed them together under the rush of icy water, watching the basin turn red, and then pink, and then clear. I kept washing my hands until they, too, felt numb.

Every so often a spasm shot through my legs and my arms would twitch, no doubt a by-product of running and running until an ache had settled so far into my body that every step had jarred my bones. My eyes kept flicking to the garden spade as if I needed to assure myself that it was still within reach. I'd placed it on the edge of the sink, but it didn't feel like it was close enough.

Turning off the faucet, I picked it up and slid it under the waistband of my jeans. The sharp edges bit into the flesh of my hip, but I tugged my shirt down over it, welcoming the little stab of pain.

I left the dingy bathroom, walking in no particular direction. The back of my shirt was soaked with sweat and my legs protested the whole walking thing. I'd take a few steps, touch the handle of the spade through my shirt, walk some more and repeat.

Take the money and run…

But run where? Where was I supposed to go? We didn't have any close friends that we'd trusted with the truth. The mortal part urged me to go to the police, but what could I say to them? By now, someone would have called 911 and her body would've been found. Then what?

If I went to the authorities, I'd be placed in the state system even though I was seventeen. We'd exhausted all of our money in the last three years and there were no funds left over except the few hundred dollars in my pocket. Lately, my mom had taken to using compulsions to get cheaper rates whenever we'd had bills to pay.

I kept walking as my brain tried to answer the question of what happens now? The sun was beginning to set. I could only hope the humidity would ease off some. My throat felt like I'd swallowed a dry sponge and my stomach grumbled unhappily. I ignored them both, continuing to put as much distance between my house and me as I could.

Where to go?

Like a sucker punch in the stomach, I saw my mom. Not how she'd looked last night, when she'd told me she loved me, that image of her escaped me. Now I kept seeing her dulled, green eyes.

A sharp stab of pain caused my step to falter. The ache in my chest, in my soul, threatened to consume me. I can't do this. Not without her.

I had to do this.

In spite of the humidity and heat, I shivered. Wrapping my arms around my chest, I barreled down the street, scanning the crowds for the horrific face of a daimon. Several seconds would pass before the elemental magic they wielded would have an effect on me. It might give me enough time to make a run for it, but they obviously could sense the little aether I had in me. It didn't seem likely that they'd follow me; daimons didn't actively hunt half-bloods. They'd tag and drain us if they happened across us, but they wouldn't seek us out. The diluted aether in us wasn't as appealing as that of the pures.

I wandered the streets aimlessly until I spied a motel that looked somewhat decent. I needed to get off the streets before nightfall. Miami after dark wasn't a place a lone, teenage girl skipped around happily.

After grabbing some burgers from a nearby fast food joint, I checked in at the motel. The guy behind the counter didn't look twice at the sweaty girl standing in front of him—with no luggage and only a bag of food—asking for a room. As long as I paid in cash, he didn't even care that I didn't show any ID.

My room was on the first floor at the end of a narrow, musty hallway. There were questionable sounds coming from some of the rooms, but I was more disturbed by the dirty carpet than the low moans.

The bottoms of my worn sneakers looked cleaner.

I shuffled the burgers and drink to my other arm as I opened the door to room 13. The irony of the number didn't pass me by; I was just too tired and out of it to care.

Surprisingly, the room smelled good, courtesy of the peach air freshener plugged into the wall outlet. I set my stuff down on the small table and pulled out the garden spade. Lifting my shirt, I inched down the band of my pants and ran my fingers over the indentations the blade had left in my skin.

It could be worse. I could be like my mo—

"Stop it!" I hissed at myself. "Just stop it."

But the aching pain welled up anyway. It was like feeling nothing and everything all at once. I drew in a shallow breath, but it hurt. Seeing my mom lying beside the bed still didn't seem real. None of this did. I kept expecting to wake up and find that everything had been a nightmare.

I just hadn't woken up yet.

I rubbed my hands on my face. There was a burning in the back of my throat, a tightness that made it hard to swallow. She's gone. She's gone. My mom's gone. I grabbed the bag of burgers and ripped into them. I ate them angrily, stopping every couple of mouthfuls to take a huge gulp from my cup. After the second one, my stomach cramped. I dropped the wrapper and rushed toward the bathroom. Falling to my knees in front of the toilet, everything came back up.

My sides ached by the time I fell back against the wall, pushing the heels of my palms against my burning eyes. Every couple of seconds my mom's blank stare flashed up, alternating with the look on the daimon's face before he'd burst into blue powder. I opened my eyes, but I still saw her, saw the blood that'd run over the purple petals, saw the blood everywhere. My arms started to tremble.

I can't do this.

I pulled my knees to my chest and rested my head on them. I slowly rocked, replaying not just the last twenty-four hours over and over again, but the last three years. All those times I'd had a chance to figure out a way to contact the Covenant and hadn't. Missed opportunities. Chances I'd never get back. I could've tried to figure out how to reach the Covenant. One call would've prevented this from happening.

I wanted a do-over—just one more day to confront my mom and demand we go back to the Covenant and face whatever had sent us fleeing in the middle of the night.

Together—we could've done it together.

My fingers dug into my hair and I pulled. A tiny cry worked its way past my clenched jaw. I yanked on my hair, but the hot flash of pain zinging across my scalp did nothing to relieve the pressure in my chest or the yawning emptiness that filled me.

As a half-blood it was my duty to kill daimons, to protect the pure-bloods from them. I'd failed in the worst way possible. I'd failed my mother. There was no way around that.

I had failed.

And I had run.

My muscles locked up and I felt a sudden rush of fury rise inside me. Balling my hands over my eyes, I kicked out. The heel of my sneaker slammed through the cabinet door below the sink. I pulled my foot free, almost pleased when the cheap particle board scraped my ankle. And I did it again and again.

When I finally did stand and leave the bathroom, the motel room was pitched in darkness. I tugged the chain on the lamp and grabbed the spade. Each step back into the shabby room hurt after forcing my sore muscles into such a cramped position in the bathroom. I sat down on the bed, not meaning to collapse there and not get back up. I'd wanted to check the door again—maybe block it with something—but exhaustion claimed me and I drifted off into a place where I hoped no nightmares could follow me.

CHAPTER 8

NIGHT TURNED TO DAY, AND I DIDN'T MOVE UNTIL THE
motel manager knocked on the door, asking for more money or for me
to get out. Through a tiny crack in the door, I handed him the cash and
went back to the bed.

I went on repeat for days. There was a general sense of time changing
when I would get up and wobble into the bathroom. I didn't have the
energy to shower, and this wasn't the kind of place that put out little
bottles of shampoo, anyway. There wasn't even a mirror in here, just a
couple of little plastic brackets framing an empty rectangle above the
sink. Either moonlight or sunshine would break through the window,
and I kept count of each time the manager visited. Three times he'd
come to ask for money.

During those days I thought of my mom and I cried until I gagged
into my hand. The storm inside me thrashed, threatening to pull me
under, and under I went. I curled up in a small ball, not wanting to talk,
not wanting to eat. Part of me just wanted to lie there and fade away.
The tears had long since come to an unsatisfying end and I just lay there,
searching for a way out. There seemed to be an empty void looming up
ahead. I welcomed it, rushed in, and sank into its meaningless depths
until the manager came the fourth day.

This time he spoke to me after I handed him the cash. "You need
something, kid?"

I stared at him through the gap. He was an older guy, maybe in his late forties. He seemed to wear the same pinstriped shirt every day, but it looked clean.

He glanced down the hall, running a hand through thinning brown hair. "Is there anyone I can call for you?"

I didn't have anyone.

"Well, if you need something, just call the front desk." He backed away, taking my silence as the answer. "Ask for Fred. That's me."

"Fred," I repeated slowly, sounding like an idiot.

Fred stalled, shaking his head. When he looked back at me, his eyes met mine. "I don't know what kind of trouble you got yourself in, kid, but you're too young to be out here and in a place like this. Go home. Go back to where you belong."

I watched Fred leave and I shut the door behind him, locking it. I turned around slowly and stared at the bed—at the garden spade. My fingers tingled.

Go back to where you belong.

I didn't belong anywhere. Mom was gone now and—

I pushed away from the door, approaching the bed. I picked up the spade and ran my fingers along the sharp edges. Go back to where you belong. There was only one place I did belong and it wasn't curled up in ball on a bed in a craptastic motel on the wrong side of Miami.

Go to the Covenant.

A tingle ran along the back of my neck. The Covenant? Could I seriously go back there after three years, not even knowing why we'd left? Mom had acted like it wasn't safe there for us, but I always chalked that up to her paranoia. Would they allow me back without my mother? Would I be punished for running away with her and not turning her in? Was I fated to become what I'd avoided all those years ago when I'd gone before the Council and punt-kicked an old lady?

They could force me into servitude.

All those risks were better than being chomped on by a daimon, better than tucking my tail between my legs and giving up. I'd never given up on anything in my entire life. I couldn't start now, not when my life seriously depended on me not losing it.

And by the way the bed looked and how I smelled, I was officially losing it.

What would my mom say if she could see me now? I doubted she'd suggest the Covenant, but she wouldn't have wanted me to give up. Doing so was a disgrace to everything she'd stood for, and to her love.

I couldn't give up.

The storm inside me stilled and the plan began to form. The closest Covenant was in Nashville, Tennessee. I didn't know exactly where, but the whole city would be swarming with Sentinels and Guards. We'd be able to sense each other—the aether always called out to us, stronger from the pures, more subtly from the halfs. I'd have to find a ride, because my butt wasn't walking all the way to Tennessee. I still had enough money to get a ticket on one of those buses I usually wouldn't consider riding in. The terminal downtown had been closed ages ago and the nearest bus stop going out of state was at the airport.

That was one hell of a hike from here.

I glanced at the bathroom. No light shone through the window. It was night again. Tomorrow morning I could take a cab to the airport and get on one of the buses. I sat down, almost smiling.

I had a plan, a crazy one that may end up backfiring on me, but it was better than giving up and doing nothing. A plan was something and it gave me hope.

After waiting until dawn, I caught a cab to the airport and lingered in the near-vacant bus terminal. The only company I had was an elderly black man cleaning the hard plastic seats and the rats that scurried along the darker corridors.

Neither were very talkative.

I pulled my legs up on the seat, cradling the spade in my lap while I forced myself to stay alert. After existing in the void of nothingness for days, I still wanted to climb into my favorite jammies and curl up in my mom's bed. If it wasn't for every little noise causing me to jump out of my seat, I would've fallen out of my chair in a dead sleep.

A handful of people were waiting for the bus when the sun rose outside the windows.

Everyone avoided me, probably because I looked like a hot mess. The motel shower hadn't even been working when I'd finally tried it, and my quick rinsing in the sink hadn't included soap or shampoo. Standing slowly, I waited until everyone got in line and looked down at the clothes I'd been wearing for days. The knees of my jeans had been torn open and the frayed edges were stained red. A sharp pang hit me in my stomach.

Pulling myself together, I climbed the steps to the bus and briefly made eye contact with the bus driver. Right away, I wished I hadn't. With a head full of bushy white hair and bifocals perched on his ruddy nose, the driver looked older than the guy who'd been cleaning the chairs. He even had an AARP sticker on the sun visor and wore suspenders. Suspenders?

Gods, there was a good chance Santa Claus was going to fall asleep at the wheel and we all were going to die.

Dragging my feet, I picked a spot in the middle and sat down beside a window. Luckily, the bus wasn't even half full and so the body odor usually associated with these buses was below the norm.

I think I was the only one who smelled.

And I did smell. A lady a few seats ahead of me turned around, wrinkling her nose. When her gaze landed on me, I looked away quickly.

Understanding my questionable hygiene was the least of my problems, it still made my cheeks burn with humiliation. How at a time like this could I even care about how I looked or smelled? I shouldn't, but I did. I didn't want to be the stinky girl on the bus. My embarrassment flashed me back to another horrendously mortifying moment in my life.

I'd been thirteen and just started an offensive training class at the Covenant. I remembered being thrilled to do something other than running and practicing blocking techniques. Caleb Nicolo—my best friend and an all around awesome guy—and I had spent the beginning of the first class pushing each other around and acting like monkeys on crack.

We'd been quite… uncontrollable when together.

Instructor Banks, an older half-blood who'd been injured while doing his Sentinel duties, had been teaching the class. He'd informed us that we'd be practicing takedowns and paired me up with a boy named Nick. Instructor Banks had shown us several times how to do it correctly, warning us that, "It has to be done this way. If not, you could break someone's neck, and that's not something I'm teaching today."

It had looked so easy, and being the cocky little brat that I'd been, I hadn't really paid attention. I'd told Caleb, "I so have this." We'd high fived like two idiots and gone back to our partners.

Nick had executed the takedown perfectly, sweeping out the leg while maintaining control of my arms. Instructor Banks had praised him. When it came to my turn, Nick had smiled and waited. Halfway through the maneuver, my grip had slipped on Nick's arm and I'd dropped him on his neck.

Not good.

When he didn't get up right away and had started moaning and twitching, I'd known I'd made a terrible miscalculation concerning my skill level. I'd put Nick's butt in the infirmary for a week and had been called the "Pile Driver" for several months after that.

Up until now, I'd never been so embarrassed in my life. I wasn't sure which humiliation was worse, though—failing in front of my peers or smelling like gym socks left forgotten in the hamper.

Sighing, I glanced down at my travel itinerary. There were two transfers: one in Orlando and the other in Atlanta. Hopefully one of those stops had some place I could clean up a little better and grab some food. Maybe they'd also have drivers who weren't nearing their expiration dates.

I looked around the bus, smothering my yawn with my hand. There were definitely no daimons on the bus; I imagined they'd loathe public transportation. And—from what I could tell—I didn't see any possible serial killers who looked like they'd prey on dirty chicks. I pulled the spade out and shoved it between me and the seat. I dozed off pretty quickly and woke up a few hours in, my neck cramping something fierce.

A couple of the people on the bus had these neat little pillows I'd have given my left arm for. Wiggling in my seat until I found a position that didn't feel like I was cramped in a cage, I didn't notice I had company until I lifted my eyes.

The woman who'd sniffed the air earlier stood in the aisle beside my seat. My gaze fell over her neatly coiffed brown hair and pressed khaki pants, not sure what to make of her. Had I stunk up the bus?

Smiling tightly, she pulled her hand out from behind her back and held a package of crackers out toward me. They were the kind with peanut butter in the middle, six to a pack. My stomach roared to life.

I blinked slowly, confused.

She shook her head, and I noticed the cross dangling from a gold chain around her neck. "I thought… you might be hungry?"

Pride sparked in my chest. The lady thought I was some homeless kid. Wait. I AM a homeless kid. I swallowed the sudden lump in my throat.

The lady's hand shook a bit as she pulled back. "You don't have to. If you change—"

"Wait," I said hoarsely, wincing at the sound of my own voice. I cleared my throat while my cheeks heated. "I'll take it. Thank… thank you."

My fingers looked especially grubby next to hers even though I'd scrubbed them in the motel bathroom. I started to thank her again, but she'd already moved back to her seat. I stared down at the package of crackers, feeling a tightening in my chest and jaw. Somewhere I'd read once that was a symptom of a heart attack, but I doubted that was what was wrong with me.

Squeezing my eyes shut, I tore into the package, eating so fast I really couldn't taste anything. Then again, it was hard to savor the first food I'd eaten in days when tears clogged my throat.

CHAPTER 9

AT THE TRANSFER IN ORLANDO, I HAD SEVERAL HOURS to try to clean up and grab some food. When the bathroom was free and it didn't look like anyone would be coming in, I locked the door and approached the sink. It was hard to look at myself in the mirror, so I avoided doing so. I stripped off my shirt, holding in a whimper as several sore muscles pulled. Choosing to ignore the fact I was kind of taking a bath in a public restroom, I grabbed a handful of rough, brown towels that were sure to make my skin break out. Dampening them and using the generic soap, I cleaned up as quickly as possible. Ghosts of deep purple bruises still marred the skin from my bra to my hip. The scratches on my back—inflicted when I'd wiggled through my mother's bedroom window—weren't as bad as I thought they'd be.

All in all, I wasn't that bad off.

I was able to score a bottle of water and some chips from a vending machine before boarding the next bus. Seeing the remarkably younger driver made me feel so much more relieved, since it was starting to get dark out. The bus was fuller than the one from Miami had been, and I was unable to fall back asleep. I just sat and stared out the window, running my fingers along the edge of the spade. My brain kind of clicked off after I finished the bag of chips and I ended up staring at the college-aged boy several rows ahead. He had an iPod, and I was jealous. I really didn't think about anything during the next five or so hours.

It was around two in the morning when we unloaded at Atlanta, arriving ahead of schedule. Georgia's air was just as thick with humidity as Florida's had been, but there was a smell of rain. The station was in some kind of industrial park surrounded by fields and long forgotten warehouses. We seemed to be on the outskirts of Atlanta, because the dazzling glow of city lights appeared a couple of miles away.

Rubbing my aching neck, I shuffled into the station. A few people had cars there waiting for them. I watched college boy rush over to a sedan and a tired-looking but happy middle-aged man climbed out and hugged him. Before my chest could tighten again, I turned away to seek out another vending machine to raid.

It took me several minutes to find the vending machines. Unlike the ones in Orlando, these were all the way back near the bathrooms, which I found gross. I pulled out the wad of cash and separated a few singles from the hundreds.

A shuffling sound, like pants dragging along the floor, caught my attention. I looked over my shoulder, scanning the dimly lit corridor. Up ahead, I could see the glass windows of the waiting room. After freezing to listen for several moments before I dismissed the sound, I turned back to the machine, grabbed another bottle of water and another bag of chips.

The idea of sitting for the next few hours made me want to break something, so I took my meager goodies and headed back outside. I kind of liked the wet smell in the air and the idea of getting rained on wasn't too bad. It would be like a natural shower of sorts. Munching on my chips, I headed around the terminal and past a rest stop full of truckers. None of them whistled or propositioned me when they saw me.

This, in a way, totally ruined my whole image of them.

Across from the rest stop turnoff were more factories. They looked like something straight out of a haunted house reality TV show—broken or boarded up windows, weeds overflowing the cracked pavement, and vines trailing up along the walls. Before Matt had decided I was a giant freak, we'd gone to one of those carnival haunted houses. Come to think of it, I should have known he'd be a wuss. He'd screamed like a girl when the guy had come out at the end and chased us with a chainsaw.

Smiling to myself, I followed a narrow path around the rest stop and tossed my empty bottle and bag into a trash bin. The sky was full of heavy clouds and the loud purr of the tractor's engines was comforting in an odd way. In four hours I'd be in Nashville. Four more hours and I'd find—

The sound of breaking glass startled me. My heart leapt in my throat. I whirled around, expecting to be faced with a horde of daimons. Instead of found two young guys. One had thrown a rock through the window of a maintenance building.

What rebels, I thought.

I moved my hand away from where I had the spade shoved into the back of my pants, studying them. They weren't much older—or cleaner—than me. One was wearing a red beanie… in May. I wondered if there was some kind of weather situation I was unaware of. My gaze drifted to his partner, whose eyes kept bouncing from his friend to me.

And that made me nervous.

Beanie boy smiled. The off-white shirt he wore clung to his scrawny frame. He didn't look like he was getting three square meals a day. Neither did his friend. "How ya doin'?"

I bit my lip. "Good. You?"

His friend gave a sharp, high-pitched laugh. "We're doing okay."

Knots began to form in my stomach. Taking a deep breath, I started to edge around them. "Well… I've got a bus to catch."

Giggles shot a quick look at Beanie Boy, and damn, Beanie Boy could book it. Within a second, he was standing in front of me and had a knife pointed right at my throat.

"We saw ya with the money back at those machines," said Beanie Boy, "and we want it."

I almost couldn't believe it. On top of everything, I was being robbed. It was official. The gods hated me.

And I hated them.

CHAPTER 10

IN STUNNED DISBELIEF, I LIFTED MY HANDS ABOVE MY head and exhaled slowly.

The one without the knife gaped at his partner. "Man, what are you doing? Why'd you pull a knife? She's just a girl. She's not going to fight us."

"Shut up. I'm running this show." Beanie Boy grabbed my arm as he leered in my face, pressing the tip of the knife under my chin.

"This wasn't part of the plan!" argued the guy who didn't seem to want to stab me. I eyed him hopefully, but he was staring at his partner, his hands opening and closing at his sides.

Great, I thought, I'm being robbed by unorganized criminals. Someone's definitely getting stabbed and it's probably going to be me. Instead of fear, I felt a hot stab of annoyance. I so did not have the time for this crap. I had a bus to catch, and hopefully, a life to reclaim.

"We saw ya getting the food." He inched the tip of the knife down my throat. "We know ya have money. A whole wad of cash, right, John? Must be a lot of hooking to get that kinda money."

I wanted to kick myself in the face. I should've been more careful. I couldn't pull out a wad of cash and expect not to be robbed. Surviving a daimon attack only to have my throat slashed for a few hundred dollars? Dammit, people sucked.

"Did ya hear me?"

I narrowed my eyes, figuring I was about five seconds from going ballistic. "Yeah, I heard you."

His fingers dug in my skin. "Then give us the damn money!"

"You're going to have to get it yourself." My gaze went to his friend. "And I dare you to try it."

Beanie Boy motioned toward John. "Get the money out of her pocket."

His partner's eyes darted between his friend and me. I hoped he refused, because he was so going to regret it if he didn't. That wad of cash was all that I had. In it was my ticket for the next bus. No one was getting that.

"Which pocket?" the one holding me asked. When I didn't answer, he shook me, and that was it.

My bitch switch was flipped and, well, my sense of self-preservation went right out the window. Everything—everything that'd happened boiled up inside me and burst. Did these wannabe gangstas actually think I was afraid of them? After everything I'd seen? My universe went red. I was going to stomp the ever-loving crap out of them.

I laughed in Beanie Boy's face.

Bewildered by my response, he lowered the knife a fraction of an inch.

"Are you freaking serious?" I wrenched my arm free and grabbed the knife from his fingers. "You're going to rob me?" I pointed the knife at him, half tempted to prick him with it. "Me?"

"Whoa, now." John backed up.

"Exactly," I waved the knife around. "If you want your bal—"

A shiver went down my spine, icy and foreboding. An innate sense kicked in and every fiber of my being screamed out a warning. It was the same thing I'd felt before I'd spotted the daimon from the balcony. Panic punched a hole in my chest.

No. They can't be here. They can't.

But I knew they were. The daimons had found me. What I couldn't wrap my head around was why they had. I was just a freaking half-blood. I wasn't even a snack pack to them. Worse yet, I was like Chinese food to them—they were going to be craving aether again in a few hours. Their time would be better spent hunting down pures. Not me. Not a half-blood.

Clearly distracted, Beanie Boy took advantage. He shot forward, grabbing and twisting my arm until I dropped the knife in his waiting hand. "You stupid bitch," he hissed in my face.

I pushed him with my free hand as I scanned the area. "You have to go! You need to go now!"

Beanie Boy pushed back and I stumbled to the side. "I'm done messing with you. Give us the money or else!"

I gained my balance, realizing these two were too stupid to live. So was I for hanging around and trying to convince them. "You don't understand. You have to go now. They're here!"

"What's she talking about?" John turned around and scanned the darkness. "Who's coming? Red, I think we should—"

"Shut up," Red said. Light from the moon broke free from the heavy clouds, glinting off the blade he jabbed at his friend. "She's just trying to freak us out."

Part of me wanted to bolt and let them deal with what I knew was coming, but I couldn't. They were mortals—obscenely stupid mortals who'd pulled a knife on me—but there was no way they deserved the kind of death coming their way. Robbery attempt or not, I couldn't let this happen. "The things that are coming are going to kill you. I'm not try—"

"Shut up!" yelled Red, swinging on me. Once again the knife was at my throat. "Just shut up!"

I looked at John, the saner of the two. "Please. You've got to listen to me! You need to go and you need to make your friend go. Now."

"Don't even think it, John," warned Red. "Now get over here and get this money!"

Desperate to get them out of here, I dug in my pocket and pulled out the wad of cash. Without thinking, I shoved it at Red's chest. "Here— take it! Just take it and go while you still can! Go!"

Red looked down, his mouth dropping open. "What the—"

A cold, arrogant laugh froze the blood in my veins. Red whirled around, squinting into the darkness. It was almost like the daimon materialized out of the shadows, because the spot had been empty a second ago. He stood a few feet from the building, his head cocked to the side and his horrific face twisted into a gruesome smile. To the boys, he looked like a yuppie in Gap jeans and a polo shirt—an easy target.

I recognized him as the daimon I'd hit over the head with a lamp.

"This is it?" John looked at Red, visibly relieved. "Man, we hit the lotto tonight."

"Run," I urged quietly, reaching behind me and wrapping my fingers around the handle of the garden spade. "Run as fast as you can."

Red glanced over his shoulder at me, snickering. "Is this your pimp?"

I couldn't even respond to that. I zeroed in on the daimon, my heart doubling over as he took a slow, lazy step forward. Something wasn't right about the daimon. It was… too calm. When the elemental magic took over, amusement flickered over his arresting features.

Then, when I was pretty sure I couldn't be having a crappier week, a second daimon stepped out of the shadows… and behind her stood another daimon.

I was so screwed.

CHAPTER 11

MY HAND WAS STILL UP IN THE AIR, CLENCHING THE four hundred and twenty five dollars along with my bus ticket. Perhaps it was shock that held me in that position. My brain quickly flipped through my lessons at the Covenant, the ones teaching us about pure-bloods who'd tasted aether and turned to the proverbial dark side.

Lesson number one: they didn't work well together.

Wrong.

Lesson number two: they didn't travel in packs.

Wrong again.

Lesson number three: they didn't share their food.

Wrong again.

And lesson number four: they didn't hunt half-bloods.

I was so going to kick a Covenant Instructor in the face if I ever made it back there alive.

John took a step back. "Too many people at this—"

The first daimon held up his hand and a gust of wind came rushing from the field behind the trio. It shot down the dirt path, slamming into John's chest, sending him flying through the air. John hit the back of the rest stop, his surprised shriek cut off by the snapping of his bones. He fell into the shrubs, a dark, lifeless lump.

Red tried to move, but the wind was still coming. It pushed him back and knocked my arm down. It was like being caught in an invisible tornado. Hundred dollar bills, a bunch of singles, and my bus ticket flew up in the air, caught and tossed by the wind. A hole opened in my chest as the rushing wind took them up and up. It was almost as if the daimons knew that, without those things, I was trapped. Completely, freaking trapped.

Lesson number five: They could still control the elements.

At least the Covenant Instructors had gotten that part right.

"What's going on?" Red backed up, stumbling over his own feet. "What the hell is going on?"

"You're going to die," said the daimon in Gap jeans. "That's what's going on."

I reached out, grabbing Red's flailing arm. "Come on! You've got to run!"

Fear rooted Red to the spot. I pulled on his arm until he twisted around. Then we were running, me and the guy who'd held a knife to my throat moments before. Flat laughter followed us as our feet left the dirt path and crashed through field grass.

"Run!" I yelled, pumping my legs until they burned. "Run! RUN!"

Red was so much slower than I was and he fell—a lot. I briefly considered leaving him there to fend for himself, but my mother hadn't raised me that way. Neither had the Covenant. I yanked him back to his feet, half tugging him across the field. Incoherent babbling came from him as I dragged him on. He was praying and crying—sobbing really. Lightning zipped overhead and a crash of thunder jolted both of us. Another bolt of light split the dark sky.

Through the fog rolling over the field, I could make out the shapes of more warehouses beyond a cluster of ancient maples. We had to make it there. We could lose them, or at least we could try. Anywhere was better than being out in the open. I pushed harder—pulled on Red harder. Our shoes tripped in the tangled weeds and my chest was hurting, the muscles in my arm straining to keep Red on his feet.

"Move," I gasped as we dashed under the canopy of trees, darting to the right. It seemed better than running in a straight line. "Keep moving."

Red finally fell in step beside me. The beanie was gone, revealing a head full of thick dreads. We dipped around a tree, both of us stumbling over thick roots and underbrush. Low hanging branches slapped at us, tearing at our clothing. But we kept running.

"What… are they?" Red asked breathlessly.

"Death," I said, knowing no better way to describe them to a mortal. Red whimpered. I think he knew I wasn't kidding.

It came out of nowhere then, slamming into us with the ferocity of a freight train. I hit the ground face first, inhaling spit and dirt. Somehow I kept ahold of the spade and rolled onto my back, praying we'd just gotten tackled by a chupacabra or a minotaur. Right now either would be far better than the alternative.

And I was not that lucky.

I stared up at the daimon as he picked Red up and held him several feet off the ground with one hand. Thrashing wildly, Red screamed as the daimon smiled, although he didn't see the rows of razor teeth that I could. Full of panic and terror, I rolled to my feet and rushed the daimon.

Before I could reach them, the daimon drew back his free arm and a burst of flames encompassed his hand. The elemental fire burned unnaturally bright, but the gaping eyeholes remained dark. Seemingly indifferent to the horror playing out across Red's face and his terrified screams, the daimon placed his fiery hand on Red's cheek. The fire sparked from the daimon's hand, swallowing Red's face and body within seconds. Red shrieked until his voice cut off, his body nothing but flames.

I stumbled backward, choking on a silent scream. The taste of bile filled my mouth.

The daimon dropped Red's corpse to the ground. The moment his hands left the body, the flames vanished. He turned to me and laughed as the elemental magic cloaked his true form.

My brain refused to accept reality. He wasn't the daimon from Miami or the one who had spoken behind the rest stop. A fourth. There were four of them—four daimons. Panic raked at me with fresh, sharp claws.

My heart pounded fiercely as I backed up, feeling a cold desperation well up inside me. I whirled around and found him now standing in front of me. Nothing moved as fast as a daimon, I realized. Not even me.

He winked.

I darted to the side, but he mimicked my movements. He shadowed each step I took and laughed at my pathetic attempts to get around him.

Then he stilled, letting his hands fall harmlessly to his sides. "Poor, little half-blood, there is nothing you can do. You can't escape us."

I clenched the handle of the spade, unable to speak as he stepped to the side.

"Run, half-blood." The daimon tilted his head toward me. "I'll enjoy the chase. And once I catch you, even the gods won't be able to stop what I will do to you. Run!"

I took off. No matter how much air I dragged into my lungs as I ran, it didn't seem like I could breathe. All I could think as branches snagged strands of my hair was that I didn't want to die like that. Not like that. Oh, gods—not like that.

The ground become uneven; each step sent a spike of pain up my leg and through my hips. I broke free from the trees as another rumble of thunder drowned out every sound except that of the blood pounding in my temples. Seeing the outline of the warehouses, I pushed my sore muscles harder. My sneakers left the weed-covered earth and pounded across a thin layer of gravel. I darted between the buildings, knowing wherever I went I might have only a few stolen moments of safety.

One of the buildings, the furthest from the woods, was several stories tall while the rest looked squat in comparison. The windows on the ground floor were either broken or boarded up. I slowed down, peering over my shoulder before I tried the door. I kicked at the rust-frozen handle and the surrounding wood cracked and gave way. I ducked inside and shut the door behind me.

My eyes roamed the dark interior, searching for something to secure the door with. It took several seconds for my eyes to adjust, and when they did, I could make out the shapes of abandoned work benches, presses, and a set of stairs. I struggled to get my fingers to stop shaking as I shoved the spade back into my pants. Grabbing a work bench, I yanked it toward the door. The screeching sound it made reminded me too much of a daimon's howl, and it also seemed to send things scurrying in the shadows. Once I'd barricaded the door, I rushed the stairs. They creaked and shifted under my weight as I took the steps two at a time, keeping a death grip on the metal railing. On the third floor, I went straight to a room with a large set of windows, dodging discarded benches and flattened boxes. A startling realization hit me as I peered out the window frantically, scouring the ground for daimons.

If I didn't make it to Nashville—if I ended up dead tonight—no one would even know. No one would even miss me or care. My face wouldn't even end up on the back of a milk carton.

I flipped out.

Leaving the room, I hit the rickety stairs and kept climbing until I reached the top floor. I raced through the dark hallway, ignoring the startled squeaks. I threw open the door and tumbled onto the roof. The storm continued violently overhead as if it had become a part of me. Lightning streaked across the sky, and a crack of thunder vibrated through my core, mocking the cyclone of emotions building inside.

Going to the edge of the roof, I peered through the fog. My eyes scanned every inch of the nearby woods and grounds where I'd just been. When I saw nothing I rushed to each of the other sides and did the same.

The daimons hadn't followed me.

Maybe they were playing with me instead, wanting me to believe I'd somehow outsmarted them. I knew they could still be out there, toying with me like a cat does with a mouse before it pounces and it rips the poor thing apart.

I went back to the center of the roof, the wind whipping my hair around my face. Lightning flashed overhead, casting my long shadow across the rooftop. Waves of sorrow crashed over me, coupled with anger and frustration. Each swell cut me from the inside, lancing open wounds that would never really heal. Bending over, I covered my mouth with both hands and screamed just as the thunder rolled through the dark clouds.

"This isn't it." My voice was a hoarse whisper. "This can't be it."

I straightened, swallowing down the burning lump in my throat. "Screw you. Screw all of you! I'm not dying like this. Not in this state, not in this stupid city and sure as hell not in this pile of crap!"

Fierce determination—so hot and full of rage—burned through my veins as I climbed back down the stairs and to the room with the windows. I dropped down on a pile of flattened boxes. Pulling my legs up to my chest, I leaned my head back against the wall. Dust coated my damp skin and clothing, sucking most of the moisture out.

I did the only thing I could do, because this couldn't be the end for me. With no money and no bus ticket, I might be trapped here for a while, but this wasn't how I was going to go out. I refused to even entertain the possibility. Closing my eyes, I knew I couldn't hide here forever.

I ran my fingers over the edge of the blade, preparing myself for what I would have to do when the daimons came. I couldn't run anymore. This was it. The sounds of the storm melted away, leaving a cloying humidity, and off in the distance, I could hear the roar of the trucks passing in the night. Life went on outside these walls. It couldn't be any different inside them.

I will survive this.

Keep reading for a sneak peek of...

Half-Blood

A Covenant Novel by

Jennifer L. Armentrout

SPENCER HILL PRESS

CHAPTER 1

MY EYES SNAPPED OPEN AS THE FREAKISH SIXTH
sense kicked my fight or flight response into overdrive. The Georgia
humidity and the dust covering the floor made it hard to breathe. Since
I'd fled Miami, no place had been safe. This abandoned factory had
proved no different.

The daimons were here.

I could hear them on the lower level, searching each room
systematically, throwing open doors, slamming them shut. The sound
threw me back to a few days ago, when I'd pushed open the door to
Mom's bedroom. She'd been lying in a crumpled heap beside a broken
pot of hibiscus flowers. Purple petals had spilled across the floor, mixing
with the blood. The memory twisted my gut into a raw ache, but I
couldn't think about her right now.

I jumped to my feet, halting in the narrow hallway, straining to hear
how many daimons were here. Three? More? My fingers jerked around
the slim handle of the garden spade. I held it up, running my fingers
over the sharp edges plated in titanium. The act reminded me of what
needed to be done. Daimons loathed titanium. Besides decapitation—
which was *way* too gross—titanium was the only thing that would kill
them. Named after the Titans, the precious metal was poisonous to those
addicted to aether.

Somewhere in the building, a floorboard groaned and gave way. A deep howl broke the silence, starting as a low whine before hitting an intense shrill pitch. The scream sounded inhuman, sick and horrifying. Nothing in this world sounded like a daimon—a hungry daimon.

And it was close.

I darted down the hallway, my tattered sneakers pounding against the worn-out boards. Speed was in my blood, and strands of long, dirty hair streamed behind me. I rounded the corner, knowing I had only seconds—

A whoosh of stale air whirled around me as the daimon grabbed a handful of my shirt, slamming me into the wall. Dust and plaster floated through the air. Black starbursts dotted my vision as I scrambled to my feet. Those soulless, pitch black holes where eyes should have been seemed to stare at me like I was his next meal ticket.

The daimon grasped my shoulder, and I let instinct take over. I twisted around, catching the surprise flickering across his pale face seconds before I kicked. My foot connected with the side of his head. The impact sent him staggering into the opposite wall. I spun around, slamming my hand into him. Surprise turned to horror as the daimon looked down at the garden spade buried deep in his stomach. It didn't matter where we aimed. Titanium always killed a daimon.

A guttural sound escaped his gaping mouth before he exploded into a shimmery blue dust.

With the spade still in hand, I whirled around and took the steps two at a time. I ignored the ache in my hips as I sprinted across the floor. I was going to make it—I had to make it. I'd be super-pissed in the afterlife if I died a virgin in this craphole.

"Little half-blood, where are you running to?"

I stumbled to the side, falling into a large steel press. Twisting around, my heart slammed against my ribs. The daimon appeared a few feet behind me. Like the one upstairs, he looked like a freak. His mouth hung open, exposing sharp, serrated teeth and those all-black holes sent chills over my skin. They reflected no light or life, only signifying death.

His cheeks were sunken, skin unearthly pale. Veins popped out, etching over his face like inky snakes. He truly looked like something out of my worst nightmare—something demonic. Only a half-blood could see through the glamour for a few moments. Then the elemental magic took over, revealing what he used to look like. Adonis came to mind—a blond, stunning man.

"What are you doing all alone?" he asked, voice deep and alluring.

I took a step back, my eyes searching the room for an exit. Wannabe Adonis blocked my way out, and I knew I couldn't stand still for long. Daimons could still wield control over the elements. If he hit me with air or fire, I was a goner.

He laughed, the sound lacking humor and life. "Maybe if you beg— and I mean, really beg—I'll let your death be a fast one. Frankly, half-bloods don't really do it for me. Pure-bloods on the other hand," he let out a sound of pleasure, "they're like fine dining. Half-bloods? You're more like fast food."

"Come one step closer, and you'll end up like your buddy upstairs." I hoped I sounded threatening enough. Not likely. "Try me."

His brows rose. "Now you're starting to upset me. That's two of us you've killed."

"You keeping a tally or something?" My heart stopped when the floor behind me creaked. I whirled around, spotting a female daimon. She inched closer, forcing me toward the other daimon.

They were caging me in, giving no opportunity to escape. Another one shrieked somewhere in the pile of crap. Panic and fear choked me. My stomach rolled violently as my fingers trembled around the garden spade. Gods, I wanted to puke.

The ringleader advanced on me. "Do you know what I'm going to do to you?"

I swallowed and fixed a smirk on my face. "Blah. Blah. You're gonna kill me. Blah. I know."

The female's ravenous shriek cut off his response. Obviously, she was very hungry. She circled me like a vulture, ready to rip into me. My eyes narrowed on her. The hungry ones were always the stupidest—the weakest of the bunch. Legend said it was the first taste of aether—the very life force running through our blood—that possessed a pure-blood. A single taste turned one into a daimon and resulted in a lifetime of addiction. There was a good chance I could get past her. The other one… well, he was a different story.

I feinted toward the female. Like a druggie going after her fix she came right at me. The male yelled at her to stop, but it was too late. I took off in the opposite direction like an Olympic sprinter, rushing for the door I'd kicked in earlier in the night. Once outside, the odds would be back in my favor. A small window of hope sparked alive and propelled me forward.

The worst possible thing happened. A wall of flames flew up in front of me, burning through benches and shooting at least eight feet into the air. It was real. No illusion. The heat blew back at me and the fire crackled, eating through the walls.

In front of me, *he* walked right through the flames, looking every bit like a daimon hunter should. The fire did not singe his pants nor dirty his shirt. Not a single dark hair was touched by the blaze. Those cool, storm-cloud-colored eyes fixed on me.

It was him—Aiden St. Delphi.

I'd never forget his name or face. The first time I'd caught a glimpse of him standing in front of the training arena, a ridiculous crush had sprung alive. I'd been fourteen and he seventeen. The fact he was a pure-blood hadn't mattered whenever I'd spotted him around campus.

Aiden's presence could mean one thing only: the Sentinels had arrived.

Our eyes met, and then he looked over my shoulder. "Get down."

I didn't need to be told twice. Like a pro, I hit the floor. The pulse of heat shot above me, crashing into the intended target. The floor shook with the daimon's wild thrashing and her wounded screams filled the air. Only titanium would kill a daimon, but I felt confident that being burnt alive didn't feel too good.

Rising up on my elbows, I peered through my dirty hair as Aiden lowered his hand. A popping sound followed the movement, and the flames vanished as fast as they appeared. Within seconds, only the smells of burnt wood, flesh, and smoke remained.

Two more Sentinels rushed the room. I recognized one of them. Kain Poros: a half-blood a year or so older than me. Once upon a time we had trained together. Kain moved with a grace he'd never had before. He went for the female, and with one quick swoop, he thrust a long, slender dagger into the burnt flesh of her skin. She too became nothing but dust.

The other Sentinel had the air of a pure-blood to him, but I'd never seen him before. He was big—steroids big—and he zeroed in on the daimon I knew was somewhere in this factory but hadn't seen yet. Watching how he moved such a large body around so gracefully made me feel sorely inadequate, especially considering I was still lying sprawled on the floor. I dragged myself to my feet, feeling the terror-fueled adrenaline rush fade.

Without warning, my head exploded in pain as the side of my face hit the floor *hard*. Stunned and confused, it took me a moment to realize the Wannabe Adonis had gotten ahold of my legs. I twisted, but the creep sank his hands deep into my hair and yanked my head back. I dug my fingers into his skin, but it did nothing to alleviate the pressure bearing down on my neck. For a startled moment, I thought he intended to rip my head right off, but he sank razor sharp teeth into my shoulder, tearing through fabric and flesh. I screamed—*really* screamed.

I was on fire—I had to be. The draining burned through my skin; sharp pricks radiated out through every cell in my body. And even though I was only a half-blood, not chock-full of aether like a pure-blood, the daimon continued to drink my essence as though I were. It wasn't my blood he was after; he'd swallow pints of it just to get at the aether. My very spirit shifted as he dragged it into him. Pain became everything.

Suddenly, the daimon lifted his mouth. "What are you?" His whispered voice slurred the words.

There was no time to even think about that question. He was ripped off me and my body slumped forward. I rolled into a messy, bloody ball, sounding more like a wounded animal than anything remotely human. It was the first time I'd ever gotten tagged—drained by a daimon.

Over the small sounds I made, I heard a sickening crunch, and then wild shrieks, but the pain had taken over my senses. It started to pull back from my fingers, sliding its way back to my core where it still blazed. I tried to breathe through it, but *damn*...

Gentle hands rolled me onto my back, prying my fingers away from my shoulder. I stared up at Aiden.

"Are you okay? Alexandria? Please say something."

"Alex," I choked out. "Everyone calls me Alex."

He gave a short, relieved laugh. "Okay. Good. Alex, can you stand?"

I think I nodded. Every few seconds a stabbing flash of heat rocked through me, but the hurt had faded into a dull ache. "That really... sucked something bad."

Aiden managed to get one arm around me, lifting me to my feet. I swayed as he brushed back my hair and took a look at the damage. "Give it a few minutes. The pain will wear off."

Lifting my head, I looked around. Kain and the other Sentinel were frowning at nearly identical piles of blue dust. The pure-blood faced us. "That should be all of them."

Aiden nodded. "Alex, we need to go. Now. Back to the Covenant."

The Covenant? Not entirely in control of my emotions, I turned to Aiden. He wore all black—the uniform Sentinels wore. For a hot second, that girly crush resurfaced from three years ago. Aiden looked sublime, but fury stomped down that stupid crush.

The Covenant was involved in this—coming to my rescue? Where the hell had they been when one of the daimons had snuck into our house?

He took a step forward, but I didn't see him—I saw my mother's lifeless body again. The last thing she ever saw on this earth was some god-awful daimon's face and the last thing she'd ever felt… I shuddered, remembering the body-ripping pain of the daimon's tag.

Aiden took another step toward me. I reacted, a response born out of anger and pain. I launched myself at him, using moves I hadn't practiced in years. Simple things like kicks and punches were one thing, but an offensive attack was something I'd barely learned.

He caught my hand and swung me around so I faced the other direction. In a matter of seconds, he had my arms pinned, but all the pain and the sorrow rose in me, overriding any common sense. I bent forward, intent on getting enough space between us to deliver a vicious back kick.

"Don't," Aiden warned, his voice deceptively soft. "I don't want to hurt you."

My breath came out harsh and ragged. I could feel the warm blood trickling down my neck, mixing with sweat. I kept fighting even though my head swam, and the fact that Aiden held me off so easily only made my world turn red with rage.

"Whoa!" Kain yelled from the sidelines, "Alex, you know us! Don't you remember me? We aren't going to hurt you."

"Shut up!" I broke free of Aiden's grasp, dodging Kain and Mister Steroids. None of them expected me to run from them, but that's what I did.

I made it to the door leading out of the factory, dodged the broken wood and rushed outside. My feet carried me toward the field across the street. My thoughts were a complete mess. Why was I running? Hadn't I been trying to get back to the Covenant since the daimon attack in Miami?

My body didn't want to do this, but I kept running through the tall weeds and prickly bushes. Heavy footsteps sounded behind me, growing closer and closer. My vision blurred a bit, my heart thundered in my chest. I was so confused, so—

A hard body crashed into me, knocking the air right out of my lungs. I went down in a spiraling mess of legs and arms. Somehow, Aiden twisted around and took the brunt of the fall. I landed on top of him, and I stayed there for a moment before he rolled me over, pinning me down into the itchy field grass.

Panic and rage burst through me. "Now? Where were you a week ago? Where was the Covenant when my mother was being killed? Where were you?"

Aiden jerked back, eyes wide. "I'm sorry. We didn't—"

His apology only angered me further. I wanted to hurt him. I wanted to make him let me go. I wanted… I wanted… I didn't know what the hell I wanted, but I couldn't stop myself from screaming, clawing, and kicking him. Only when Aiden pressed his long, lean body against mine did I stop. His weight, the close proximity, held me immobile.

There wasn't an inch of space between us. I could feel the hard ripple of his abdominal muscles pressing against my stomach, could feel his lips only inches from mine. Suddenly I entertained a wild idea. I wondered if his lips felt as good as they looked… because they looked awesome.

That was a wrong thought to have. I had to be crazy—the only plausible excuse for what I was doing and thinking. The way I stared at his lips or the fact I desperately wanted to be kissed—all wrong for a multitude of reasons. Besides the fact I'd just tried to knock his head off, I looked like a mess. Grime dirtied my face beyond recognition; I hadn't showered in a week and I was pretty sure I smelled. I was *that* gross.

But the way he lowered his head, I really thought he was going to kiss me. My entire body tensed in anticipation, like waiting to be kissed for the first time, and this was definitely not the first time I'd been kissed. I'd kissed lots of boys, but not him.

Not a *pure-blood.*

Aiden shifted, pressing down further. I inhaled sharply and my mind raced a million miles a second, spewing out nothing helpful. He moved his right hand to my forehead. Warning bells went off.

He murmured a compulsion, fast and low, too quick for me make out the words.

Son of a—

A sudden darkness rushed me, void of thought and meaning. There was no fighting something that powerful, and without getting out so much as a word of protest, I sank into its murky depths.

A cruise ship.
A beautiful island.
Two sexy guys.

What could possibly go wrong?

In the Bermuda Triangle—a lot.

Triangles

Kimberly Ann Miller

Coming in June 2013

Life has been hell for seventeen-year-old Emma since she moved from sunny California to a remote Alaskan town. Rejected by her father and living with the guilt of causing her mother's death, she makes a desperate dash for freedom from her abusive stepfather. But when her car skids off the icy road, her escape only leads to further captivity in a world beyond her imagining.

Angela J. Townsend

Amarok

Angelina's Secret

Coming in Spring 2012 from Spencer Hill Press

As a child, Angelina spent years in counseling learning that Josie, her imaginary friend, wasn't real, but it turns out her childhood friend wasn't imaginary after all.

Lisa Rogers

978-0-9831572-8-1

Masters

of the Veil

Book One of the Veil Trilogy

There's no "I" in SORCERY.

Daniel A. Cohen

978-1-937053-02-4

PODs

A Novel

The end
of the world
is only the
beginning.

Michelle Pickett

Coming in June 2013

January 2013

Having poison running
through your veins and
a kiss that kills really
puts a dent in high school.

Kelly
Hashway

Touch of Death

Photo by Vania Stoyanova

Jennifer L. Armentrout lives in West Virginia. All the rumors you've heard about her state aren't true. Well, mostly. When she's not hard at work writing, she spends her time reading, working out, watching zombie movies, and pretending to write. She shares her home with her husband, his K-9 partner named Diesel, and her hyper Jack Russell Loki. Her dreams of becoming an author started in algebra class, where she spent her time writing short stories... therefore explaining her dismal grades in math. Jennifer writes Adult and Young Adult Urban Fantasy and Romance.

Come find out more at: **www.jenniferarmentrout.com**